JACK MARLOWE

TRULY TERRIBLE TALES

I have to escape, or die...

WRITERS

h

Hodder
Children's
Books

a division of Hodder Headline plc

Text © Jack Marlowe 1997
Illustrations © Scoular Anderson 1997

First published in 1997 by Hodder Children's Books

The right of Jack Marlowe and Scoular Anderson to be identified as the author and illustrator of this work has been asserted by them in accordance with the Copyright, Designs and Patents Act 1988.

Designed by Don Martin

10 9 8 7 6 5 4 3 2 1

A catalogue record for this book is available from the British Library.

ISBN 0 340 66724 9

Hodder Children's Books
A division of Hodder Headline plc
338 Euston Road
London
NW1 3BH

Printed and bound by Mackays of Chatham plc, Chatham, Kent

Contents

iii

Introduction

Being a writer seems such a lovely, peaceful job, doesn't it? The writer sits in front of a cosy fire with a pen and paper and scribbles away while people struggle to live in the harsh world outside. Right?

Wrong.

Writing can be dangerous! No, I don't mean the pen could slip and you could die of ink poisoning. I mean, the writer can say the wrong thing and upset

WARNING: WRITING CAN BE DANGEROUS

The game's up, pen pusher!

important people. A writer called Baron Lytton said, "The pen is mightier than the sword". He meant that writers can spread dangerous ideas with their pens.

A writer might say, "Let's get rid of the king and rule this country without him!" If everybody agrees then the king could be thrown off his throne!

Of course a clever king would not let this happen. The troublesome writers may be locked up in some dungeon and lose their pens and paper. The really unlucky writers would simply lose their heads! Baron Lytton may have said that the pen is mightier than the sword – but if I was going to fight I know which one I'd rather have!

So writers through history have scribbled their stories on stone and leather and paper and parchment. But sometimes the true stories of their lives have been more terrible than the tales they told.

SENECA

4 BC - AD 65

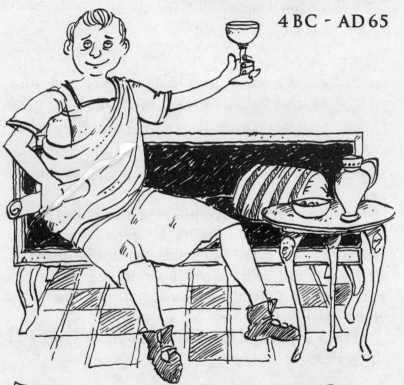

THE ROMAN ROTTER

Ancient Rome was a violent place and the writer Seneca was a dangerous man to know. He first started writing when the emperor Caligula ruled Rome. But Caligula was a vicious man - in his reign he

*   drove nine people to kill themselves,

   *   had eleven executed

     *   had a gladiator poisoned

       *   had one Roman leader starved to death and another hacked to death

         *   had an actress friend of Seneca's tortured to death.

Seneca didn't object, of course - he didn't want to be next!

Emperor Caligula loved to watch gladiators fight to the death in the arena Games. He even joined in the killing. At one event he fought against a gladiator who was armed with a wooden sword. It wasn't a fair fight because Caligula was using a real sword. Of course the gladiator died.

Seneca wrote a famous letter about the cruelty of the games:

I HAPPENED TO DROP IN ON THE MID-DAY SPORT IN THE ARENA. I WAS LOOKING FOR A LITTLE ENTERTAINMENT BUT SAW ONLY BUTCHERY, PURE AND SIMPLE. THE FIGHTERS HAVE NOTHING TO PROTECT

THEM. THEIR BODIES ARE OPEN TO EVERY
BLOW, AND EVERY BLOW FINDS ITS MARK.
THEY ARE LASHED FORWARD SO THEY
CAN'T ESCAPE THE SWORD.

IN THE MORNING MEN FIGHT LIONS AND
BEARS, AT NOON THEY FIGHT EACH OTHER.
THE WINNER FIGHTS AGAIN AND AGAIN
UNTIL HE IS DEFEATED. DEATH IS THE
FIGHTER'S ONLY WAY OUT. THE SPECTATORS
SAY, "BUT THESE MEN ARE HIGHWAY
ROBBERS AND MURDERERS. THEY DESERVE
ALL THEY ARE GETTING!" CAN'T YOU SEE
HOW WRONG THIS SPORT IS?

Emperors didn't like people writing letters like this.
Caligula could have had Seneca killed but instead he
had the writer sent off to live on the island of Corsica.
He was stuck there for eight weary years. Seneca must
have been pleased when Caligula was stabbed to
death and replaced by his uncle Claudius. Seneca
wormed his way back into favour and returned to
Rome.

The Emperor Claudius gave Seneca the job of
teaching his adopted son, Nero. Then Claudius was
poisoned - probably by his third wife, Agrippina. You
can see that being an emperor was a dangerous job in
Ancient Rome!

That's my boy!

Nero took control of the Roman Empire – but teacher Seneca had control of Nero. Seneca wrote Nero's speeches and Nero let his teacher run the empire.

Seneca did a good job at a difficult time and many people believed he brought a little kindness to the vicious Roman world – but just how kind was he?

SENECA THE ROMAN LEADER

THE ROMANS COULD BE REALLY CRUEL TO THEIR SLAVES. ONE ROMAN HAD HIS SLAVES CHOPPED UP AND FED TO HIS EELS IF THEY DID SOMETHING WRONG!

SENECA HATED SLAVERY – HE SAID. HE TRIED TO MAKE LIFE FOR THE SLAVES A

LITTLE BETTER. BUT HE DIDN'T ALWAYS GO
OUT OF HIS WAY TO HELP THEM.

THERE WAS THE TIME WHEN A SLAVE
MURDERED HIS MASTER AND SENECA WAS
ONE OF THE JUDGES WHO COULD HAVE
GONE TO THE TRIAL.

THE MURDERED ROMAN HAD 400 SLAVES
AND THE JUDGES DECIDED THAT ALL 400
SHOULD DIE, THOUGH ONLY ONE
COMMITTED THE CRIME.

SENECA DIDN'T EVEN BOTHER TO TURN UP
FOR THE TRIAL AND WAS HAPPY TO LET
THE 400 DIE.

SO MUCH FOR SENECA'S 'KINDNESS'!

While Seneca was in power there was trouble in
Britain. A lot of this was to do with the Britons suffering from Roman taxes. That was Seneca's fault. He
was a greedy man and wanted to make sure he
squeezed every last bit of money out of the beaten
Brits.

Angry Britons, led by Queen Boudicca, couldn't
get to Seneca in Rome. So they massacred the Roman
men, women and children living in Britain - then of
course the Roman army massacred the Britons in

revenge. Boudicca probably poisoned herself rather than be taken prisoner. There was an awful lot of poisoning going on in Seneca's time!

Rome was saved. Seneca grew richer and more powerful. He told Nero, "It is good to be poor." Then he went away to count his fortune. If he'd been living today he'd have been a millionaire.

Poor old me!

He made his money from money-lending, not from his writing. His writing was something he did for pleasure.

Seneca hadn't just written speeches for Nero. He'd written books and plays. His favourite subjects were crime and horror, witches and ghosts, and they were very popular. The Romans loved tales of revenge. Stories like that of the Greek witch Medea...

Medea

A TRAGIC PLAY BY SENECA

MEDEA WAS A GREEK PRINCESS. SHE
LOVED THE HERO JASON AND HELPED HIM
TO STEAL HER FATHER'S PRICELESS GOLDEN
FLEECE. THEN SHE SAILED AWAY WITH
JASON AND HER YOUNGER BROTHER.
WHEN THEY SAW HER FATHER WAS
FOLLOWING THEM, MEDEA CHOPPED UP
HER BROTHER AND THREW
THE BITS IN THE SEA.
HER FATHER STOPPED
TO PICK UP THE BITS
AND SHE ESCAPED.

Tee-hee!

WHEN SHE MET
JASON'S NEXT ENEMY
SHE TRICKED THE
MAN'S DAUGHTERS
INTO CUTTING HIM UP
AND BOILING THE
PIECES IN A POT.

JASON GREW TIRED
OF HER AFTER A FEW
YEARS AND FELL IN
LOVE WITH ANOTHER

Seneca's plays were popular long after his death in 65 AD. Fifteen hundred years later English writers like William Shakespeare used some of Seneca's ideas for their own plays. In one of his first plays William Shakespeare told the story of Titus Andronicus that was every bit as gory as a Seneca play...

8

TITUS ANDRONICUS

by William Shakespeare

Titus is a Roman hero who has just defeated a powerful enemy. He celebrates by sacrificing the son of the beaten queen to the gods - which does not make him popular with the queen, Tamora.

Titus's own daughter, Lavinia is kidnapped and has her hands cut off and her tongue cut out. Tamora accuses Titus's sons of murder but Titus is told they will be forgiven if he cuts off his own hand. He does this, but it was all a trick. His sons are executed anyway.

Titus then plots his revenge on Tamora. First he cuts the throats of Tamora's sons, while hand-less Lavinia catches their blood in a bowl. Then he bakes the boys into a pie and serves it up to Tamora. After she has eaten her sons he tells her what she has done then stabs her. He also puts Lavinia out of her misery by killing her. Finally he is killed by the dead queen's husband.

Seneca would have loved that story. It was a bit like his real life amongst the murdering emperors!

But the most truly terrible tale of all was Seneca's own foul fate. It wasn't a story of horror and revenge - it was real.

Nero turns nasty

Things started to go wrong after Nero had ruled for about five years. The emperor had an enemy called Britannicus - he had him poisoned. Nero began to enjoy his power and started to take back control of the empire from Seneca. Soon Nero was out of Seneca's control.

The next to die was Nero's mother, Agrippina - cut to pieces by Nero's soldiers.

The Roman people were horrified. So Seneca wrote a wonderful speech for Nero, explaining exactly why Agrippina had to die!

So long, Seneca

Seneca knew that Nero was a mad murderer. But what could he do to stop his old pupil's wicked ways?

Poison him, of course! Seneca supported a plot to kill Nero. Why not? Nero had probably poisoned Seneca's best friend Burrus and he even tried to poison Seneca himself! The writer enjoyed writing plays about revenge and now it was his turn to try it on Nero.

The trouble was, the poisoning plot failed. Nero found out and he was furious. He knew who the plotters were, but he didn't have Seneca executed. Instead he ordered Seneca to kill himself! Gruesome.

Seneca went back to his house, lay down on a comfortable couch and took out his sharpest knife. He then cut his wrist and slowly bled to death.

Seneca's writing had made him a powerful man. He used that power to make himself rich. He also used his writing skills to get himself out of trouble.

The old emperor, Caligula, had banished Seneca from Rome and the writer had to spend eight years on the boring island of Corsica, away from the pleasures of Rome. How did he persuade new emperor Claudius to forgive him? He wrote books about how wonderful Claudius was. What a creep!

What did he do when Claudius died? He wrote books about what a fool Claudius was.

Seneca was a very clever writer. Sadly he was not a very nice man.

Truly revolting Romans

Seneca wasn't the only ancient writer to die a dreadful death. In the Ancient Greek world there was a story-teller called Aesop. He wrote stories that have lasted to this day – stories like "The Tortoise and the Hare" and "The boy who cried Wolf".

He was also a very funny man. Aesop was sent to Delphi temple where he cracked a few jokes about the gods. The priests didn't laugh. In fact the priests were a bit annoyed. Or, rather, the priests were absolutely furious. They took the top story teller to the top storey of the temple – and threw him off.

Aesop was Ae-stopped when he hit the ground. Dead men tell no tales and Aesop told no more tales after flying with all the skill of a penguin.

Dastardly deeds

But the Roman emperors around Seneca's time were especially cruel. Seneca must have enjoyed the death of Nero's mother, Agrippina. The first plot to kill her was incredibly clever, but it failed. If Nero had drawn up a plan it might have looked like this:

I BUILD A COLLAPSIBLE BOAT THAT WILL SNAP IN HALF.

SNAP!!

← PERFORATIONS

II INVITE MOTHER TO A MEETING AND SEND THE BOAT TO FETCH HER

MESSENGER
INVITATION
MUM

MUM GETS INTO BOAT

III WHEN THE BOAT IS IN DEEP WATER, LET THE HEAVY ROOF CRASH DOWN ONTO AGRIPPINA AND THROUGH BOTTOM OF BOAT

ROOF

REALLY DEEP

WALLOP

IV HAVE SOLDIERS HANDY TO FINISH HER OFF IF SHE SURVIVES THE SHIPWRECK

SOLDIERS →

SURVIVOR

But the plan didn't work! The roof of the canopy crashed down all right but Agrippina survived and started to swim to safety. Her faithful maid saw what had happened and started screaming, "I am Agrippina! Save me! I am Agrippina, save me!" Of course the soldiers killed her! Agrippina reached the shore.

Nero tried something a bit more certain next time. He sent a friend with a very sharp sword to murder her. It worked.

By the way, don't feel too sorry for Agrippina. She probably had the old emperor, Claudius, poisoned so that her son, Nero, could become emperor.

She also had Nero's rival, Britannicus, poisoned at a children's holiday party. (Some of the children almost died too from the poisoned cakes.)

Nero's father once tore out the eye of a jockey at a horse race and ran over a child in his chariot – just for fun!

And you thought your parents were bad!

BEDE

673 - 735 AD

THE MANIC MONK

Seneca wrote books because he was bored. He'd upset Emperor Caligula and was sent to live on a boring island with nothing to do but write. So that's what he did.

Lots of writers enjoy peace and quiet to get on with their writing and one of Britain's greatest writers was a monk in the north of England called Bede.

Bede's most famous book was probably his history of the English people. The times he lived in are known as The Dark Ages because we know so little about what happened. Without Bede we'd have known even less about the English and where they came from. But he also found time to study science. He said that the Earth was a globe while most people of his time thought it was flat. He could have been right because no one has fallen off the edge – yet!

Now, life in a monastery may seem a little tame but in fact Bede's life had some moments of drama, as well as long periods when he spent time writing with a goose feather on the leather from the belly of a calf.

Life for a writing monk like Bede was not always easy. Letters still exist that tell us about the death of Bede. If there had been letters about his life then they may have looked something like this.

A string of Bede's letters

Imagine being a child of seven in Saxon times. You live near the River Wear on the cool coast of North-east England and your family share a two-roomed house. The walls are woven from branches and the

gaps are filled in with mud – or sometimes pigs' drop-
pings! Phew!

There was no chimney so the smoke swirls around
the room. It's no wonder these Anglo-Saxons suffer
from bad coughs and that half of them die by the age
of 25.

As soon as you can walk you are helping around
the farm, feeding the animals, gathering firewood or
weeding the fields.

Of course you'll have time for fun and games.
Children can play "chuckstones" using the bones from
a boiled pig's trotter. You will try your hand at knit-

19

ting (along with the rest of the family), ice-skating (on skates made of animal bones strapped to the feet) and chess (if you're rich enough to own a set or clever enough to carve one).

The adults in your village will have rather more cruel sports. They enjoy watching dogs attack a bull that was tied by a rope to a post. This often ends up with the death of the bull or the dogs.

And down on the river side is that church with the high stone walls and those strange men with shaven

heads - the monks. Bede must have been nervous when his parents sent him away from his home and his friends to live in that monastery. He was only seven years old at the time!

That was the hard life Bede's parents sent him into. But he wasn't alone. So many people wanted to be monks that the monastery was soon overflowing.

Dear Sir,

Thank you for applying to send your son, Bede, to St Peter's monastery at Wearmouth. I should explain that it will be a hard life for the boy but he will learn to read, write, pray and work. His life on earth will be hard but his path to heaven will be easier.

Your son will learn to pray seven times a day, the first service being at 2 o'clock in the morning. He will have lessons and will work in the fields between prayers. The food is simple and not too rich, mainly porridge and bread with roast flesh of birds on special occasions.

Young Bede will also learn to obey. Senior monks will beat him with sticks if he is lazy or misbehaves. He will also spend time in a cell with bread and water if he is really wicked.

All you have to do is bring him along with a linen bundle containing bread and wine for the abbot and, don't forget, some money.

Yours in faith

ABBOT BISCOP

King Ecgfrith had given land to the monks to build St Peter's monastery. Bede had just settled into the old monastery when he was sent off to help build a new one, ten miles away, in a place called Gyrwe. By then he would be eight years old and probably a skilled writer...

Dear Father and Mother,

The good King Ecgfrith has given us land on the river Tyne called Gyrwe. Today I have visited the place where we will build the new monastery and it is a grim task ahead of us. Gyrwe is an old word and I have learned that it means "swamp". Good King Ecgfrith has given us a swamp. In return he will be sure to get a seat in heaven close to God, so he has made a good bargain. We have to say prayers so he will win his battles

BEDE'S VISION

against the Mercians. It is not easy
kneeling in a turf hut on a muddy floor
to pray.

First we will have to drain the water off
the land and try to scrape a living while
the stone masons begin to build a
church. It will be called St Paul's.

It is exciting to be here and to know
we will see a church rise from the swamp.
But it is very cold and it is hard to write
with numb hands.

Your loving son,

BEDE.

Hard work, draughty, freezing rooms and poor food
would make most of us want to get back home - even
if home was a house made of pig's-dropping walls!

By 685 the 12 year-old Bede must have been start-
ing to collect the stories that added up to make his
history. In that year he would have heard the dreadful news about King Ecgfrith. The king had given land
to the monks so they would pray for him to beat the
Mercians to the south. He didn't give them land when
he set off to fight the Picts to the north. Perhaps he
should have done.

King Ecgfrith waited till the spring before he attacked his old enemies, the Picts. Those wild men were forever raiding Ecgfrith's lands and stealing his farmers' cattle. It was time to put a stop to their thieving once and for all.

A miserable march

Marching through Northern England in winter would have been slow and his men would suffer. The king celebrated Easter with his friends in the monastery then set off in the mild spring weather. He wanted to destroy the wild raiders from Pictland - the place we call Scotland today.

The army must have been eager to follow him They'd spent all winter training but the idea of a real fight against these ragged, hairy, filthy Picts kept them going. They marched through Northumberland and into the unknown hills of Scotland. The trouble was there were no Picts in sight. There were a few miserable villages in the valleys, but the people had all run away as Ecgfrith's army drew near.

They marched on. The further they marched the stranger the land became. The hills were steeper and gloomier, the winds colder and the mists thicker. And the further they marched the hungrier they became. They hadn't expected to be away from England this long. The cheerful army that set off from Northumbria was cold, tired and hungry.

A treacherous trap

The Picts knew this, of course. The ragged cattle-thieves kept moving north, deeper into the bleak hills. They didn't want to meet Ecgfrith's army in open battle. They knew they'd lose. Instead they played their own game of cat and mouse.

Then on 20 May Ecgfrith received the report he'd been longing for. The enemy were at a place called

Nechtansmere! The messenger said the quickest way was through Nechtan Pass. It was a steep climb but a battle would come at the end of their climb. The soldiers were weary from marching but Ecgfrith urged them forward, into the pass.

He wouldn't have been so eager if he'd known that the messenger was a traitor, the message was false and his army were marching into a trap.

Nechtan Pass was narrow and rocky. Ecgfrith's men walked in a single line as the mist grew colder, denser and darker. Their high spirits had gone now as the path grew steeper and the climb exhausted them.

Suddenly the men at the front came across a boulder that had been rolled across the path. It loomed out of the mist and blocked their way. They stopped, of course. The men behind collided with them.

Then they heard a rumbling as a boulder was rolled behind the men at the back of the column. Ecgfrith and his men were trapped.

Screams pierced the colourless air. The Picts swept down from their hiding places on the hill sides with savage cries and swirling skirts, more like ghosts than soldiers.

Ecgfrith and most of his men died before they could even draw their swords.

Sole survivor

Only one English man survived the slaughter. Caedmon, the king's minstrel, hid in the shelter of a rock till the last of the dying screams had faded.

Shaking and stumbling he crept out onto the blood blotted heather.

Every other man of Ecgfrith's army had been butchered. Ecgfrith's corpse was stripped of its rich armour and cut to pieces. Caedmon limped home with his tragic tale.

That was the story that Bede heard from the only survivor. That was the story that Bede wrote down for us to read.

Bede was not just writing history - he was living through it. No wonder he wanted to record these events as a writer.

But Bede stuck to his work and found in 686 that there were worse problems than the cold and the struggle to write to worry about...

Dear Abbott

Please excuse this letter. I know a 13 year-old novice should not write to an abbot but there is no one else.

A dreadful plague came to the village near St Paul's monastery - a sweating sickness. They have a terrible burning fever and awful sickness. They see dreadful nightmare visions and are dead within three days. We have many herbs and cures here in the monastery garden. Of course the villagers came to us for help. We tried our cures but most of the villagers died. Then worse followed. The monks who nursed the plague victims began to fall sick.

Yesterday Brother Edwin finally died. Abbot Alcuin and I are the last two survivors and he has asked me to write to you for your prayers and for your

help. Please will you send someone to help us to bury the dead. There are just too many corpses and too few to dig.

We may be dead by the time you receive this. God bless and save us.

NOVICE BEDE.

In fact Bede survived. It was seen as a miracle - God let the 13 year old boy live because God had special work for him.

There were even stories of another miracle. Young Bede had a stammer when he spoke. The old religious man, Saint Cuthbert, visited Bede and talked to him. Bede's stammer disappeared!

By the year 735 Bede was sixty-three years old - a fair age in Saxon times. He must have been worn out by the constant work and prayer. His health began to fail.

While we know very little about his life, Bede's death is well recorded. A young monk called Cuthbert (not the Saint), wrote a letter to a friend about Bede's death.

Bede was so important by this time that copies of the letter were sent to monasteries throughout Europe. Copies have survived, so we know the content.

These are not the exact words of Cuthbert's letter but the events are correct:

St Paul's Monastery
Jarrow
20 May, 735 AD

Dear Cuthwine,

I write to you with sad news. Our dear brother Bede has passed away quietly. For the past few months he has been tiring easily. Then, two weeks before Easter, I found he had collapsed in his cell and was struggling for breath. He said, "I am in no pain," but he was too weak to rise.

From then on a monk always stayed with Bede, day and night. Bede never stopped giving lessons. He never stopped singing hymns and praying, or working on his book, even if he was ill.

One evening we were singing our hymn, "Do not leave us, orphans without a father," when Bede started to cry. All the monks started to cry with him. It took them a long time to recover from this incident.

Over the last few weeks Bede's breathing became worse. His feet were swelling very badly. One day whilst he was teaching he said, "Learn your lessons quickly for I will not be around much longer."

This morning when day broke Bede sent for the novice Wilbert to dictate his work. He worked from 6:30 a.m. until 9:00 a.m. Wilbert said to Bede, "There is still one chapter to be finished in your book." Bede dictated it to him and Wilbert wrote it.

At 3:00 p.m. Bede sent for his most treasured possessions; incense, linen napkins and pepper which he had been saving. He saw each monk separately and shared his possessions amongst them. In the final hour of his life, Wilbert said, "You have one last sentence to write."

"Then listen carefully and write quickly," said Bede, and he recited the words.

"Now it is finished," said Wilbert.

"You have spoken true. It is finished," Bede said quietly.

Then, with our help, Bede knelt and prayed. "Glory be to the Father and the Son and the Holy Spirit." And on that word he died.

From your faithful brother,

CUTHBERT

History can be interesting when it tells us about the way people behaved. And Bede's own death is as interesting as the facts he collected in his history of England.

Imagine it. You are ill and close to death. Someone tells you there is still a chapter of your book to write. What would you say? Would you say, "You must be joking! Leave me in peace?"

Or, like Bede, would you say, "Well, let's get on with it quickly"?

What a man and what a writer!

Anglo-Saxon facts

If Bede hadn't entered the monastery what sort of life would he have led? And would you have liked to live in those times? Anglo-Saxon life sounds great! No school to suffer and no terrible teachers! But . . .

Would YOU have survived in Anglo-Saxon times?

Could you stay CLEAN?
Anglo-Saxons washed their clothes in the river. They didn't have soap powder that we do. Instead they made their own from ashes, animal fat ... and human urine!

Could you stay COMFORTABLE?
The Saxons burned their dead to ashes and put the ashes into pots to be buried, perhaps with something small like a comb. The combs that have been found have the teeth very close together. This was to drag the nits from your hair. Everyone had nits in the hair and lice on the body.

Could you stay HEALTHY?
To get rid of worms that infested their stomachs the Anglo-Saxons ate small amounts of bracken from the woods. Large amounts would kill you so you had to be careful!

Could you LIVE like a monk?

Monks shaved the top of their heads. First they cut off the hair with a small pair of shears then they rubbed the rest off with a stone - called a pumice stone - until there was no hair left on top. Rub too hard and you rubbed the skin off! Even if you survived the haircut you'd have a very cold head in winter. That's why monk's cloaks (or "habits") had hoods on.

Could you EAT the food?
Apart from eating vegetables, nuts and berries, meat and cheeses the Anglo-Saxons also ate weeds! Could you have managed a dandelion salad? Or how about nettle stew?

Could you have SLEPT at night?
You'd have to listen to those sounds in the thatched roof above you. The sounds of rats and mice in their nests!

ANOTHER QUIET NIGHT AT ST. PAUL'S

And –

Could you have written like Bede?

There were no printing machines in Bede's time. Everything had to be written carefully by hand then copied by hand. Anglo-Saxon writers used "quill" pens made from feathers and wrote on fine leather made from the stomach-skin of a calf.

Bede wrote a rough copy first which he sent to friends for criticism or comment. Then he made a better copy which he again sent out to be checked by all the experts he could find. Finally he made the published version.

Not only was he the first person to write the history of the English people, he was also the first to be so careful about checking his facts.

When he became too frail to hold a quill he spoke the words to young monks who wrote them down.

Christopher Marlowe

1564 – 1593

A MYSTERIOUS MURDER

Writers have to eat. Many try to sell their work and make enough money to live on, but not many have managed that.

Seneca was a teacher and had a rich wife. Bede was helped by the monks who worked in the monastery fields so their history writer could create his books.

But by Tudor times the monasteries were gone. Writers in Elizabethan England needed to be rich – or they needed another job to give them money while they wrote. Writers with little money lived in poor slum houses and mixed with criminals. Some spent time in jail for not paying their bills – or worse, joined the criminals in their lawless life!

The theatre in the days of Queen Elizabeth was growing more and more popular.

There was work in the theatres for playwrights, but the pay was truly terrible. The writer would be paid from £2 to £4 for the script and get nothing else. A really successful play could make £4 from one performance and the theatre owners got hundreds of pounds a year. The writer didn't get another penny.

Some writers were sensible with their money - writers like William Shakespeare bought a share of The Globe Theatre and became rich. But writers like Christopher Marlowe spent it on drinking and gambling. The drinking led them into fights and the fights led them to jail. The gambling left them poor and willing to do anything to make a little money – even spying for England in the wars against Spain.

If the Elizabethans had newspapers then they could have followed the career of Marlowe and his friends through press cuttings to his truly terrible end.

Play dead

In 1589 Christopher Marlowe was a popular playwright and a well-known poet. But he seemed to have some dangerous friends...

The Elizabethan Times

1st October 1589

FATAL FIGHT
Playwright
FREE

By Our *Special Correspondent*

TODAY playwright Christopher Marlowe (25) walked free from *Newgate jail*, cleared of the murder of William Bradley on 18 September.

"Kit" Marlowe

Marlowe, known to his friends as 'Kit', smiled as he stepped into the daylight for the first time in almost two weeks. "My friend Tom Watson and I have been held in a filthy dungeon called the Limboes," he announced. "There was just a single candle for light, rats for company and straw in the corner for a toilet. That's no way to treat two gentlemen," he complained. "We were innocent anyway," he added.

❦

Later the playwright, best known for his plays *"Tamburlaine the Great"* and *"Doctor Fausus"*, described the death of Bradley to our reporter.

"I was in a tavern in Hog Lane when William Bradley insulted me. He's an upstart innkeeper's son and I wasn't having him telling lies about me. I offered to fight him outside in Hog Lane. I wanted to teach him a lesson and maybe give him a beating. But Bradley drew his sword and attacked me. There were a lot of people came running to watch the fight and my friend Tom Watson was one of them," Marlowe said.

Watson   Bradley

Thomas Watson (33) is, of course, a popular poet and playwright who is also a science writer and student of law. Marlowe said they had been friends for two years. He went on, "Tom wanted to stop the fight. He could see I'd had a lot to drink and I wasn't too steady on my feet. Tom drew his sword and stepped between us to keep the peace. I put my sword away and stepped back. But that villain Bradley started lashing out at Tom with his sword. As you know Hog Lane is just a mud path outside the city walls and not easy to fight

on. Bradley had a sword and a dagger out and he drove Tom back to the ditch along the side of the road. Tom couldn't go back any further. He just had to start fighting back to save his life."

The point of Watson's sword pierced Bradley's chest to a depth of six inches and killed the innkeeper's son instantly. "Tom never meant to kill him!" Marlowe claimed. "But we were both arrested and thrown into that stinking hole they call Newgate jail."

An inquest was held into the death of William Bradley. Reports can be found in our edition of 19 September. The jury decided that Watson had killed Bradley in self defence. Marlowe was not guilty of any crime but had to find £40 before he could be released. It took Marlowe two weeks to raise the money which is why he stayed in prison.

Kit Marlowe was asked if he had any regrets. "Bradley was a loud-mouthed fool. I'm not sorry to see him in his grave," he replied.

Marlowe's new play, "The Jew of Malta" is being performed in the Curtain Theatre next week. ✾

A spell in a filthy dungeon would probably make you behave yourself.

A prisoner Richard Vennor described his life there.

"This prison's a fine and comfortable place . . . if you can afford it. When the Sergeants dragged me in here I paid to have my own cell. I paid for food and wine. But, when my money ran out, they threw me in 'The Hole'. Unless I can get free then I'll die in here. I sleep on bare boards with fifty other men. Wherever you look some poor soul lies groaning in sorrow - the child weeping over his dying father, the mother over her sick child. In the winter the cold will kill you - in the warmer summer weather then diseases multiply in the filth and the stinking air and kill you. If you live through the cold and sickness then the hunger will get you. The play-writer Dekker said that in The Hole you are 'buried before you are dead'. That's me, suffering a living death. My crime? I sold tickets for plays - plays that were never performed. I pocketed the money. Never let yourself be taken to prison."

Richard Vennor died.

It should have made Marlowe behave. It didn't! In 1592 he was accused of "Breach of the Peace" in Shoreditch where William Bradley had been killed. Just a few months later he was in trouble again in Canterbury for fighting. This time he wasn't so blameless.

Canterbury Herald

DECEMBER 1592

CONSTABLE'S SON IN BRAWL

LOCAL Constable, John Marlowe, had the unpleasant job of arresting his own son, Christopher (28) following a vicious street fight in Canterbury today.

Christopher Marlowe, the writer of the popular horror play *The Jew of Malta* was visiting his parents in his home town of Canterbury when the fight broke out. Tailor William Corkine (30) is accusing young Marlowe of attacking him.

Witnesses were not clear who started the fight but the playwright insists it was Corkine. The result was both men attacked one another with staffs and daggers and both received slight wounds before they were dragged apart.

Christopher Marlowe was born in this town and lived here till he went to university in Cambridge. He began writing poems and popular plays ten years ago. He is in Canterbury because the London theatres have been closed by the plague.

The people of Canterbury do not want him bringing his vicious London habits to our town. Constable John Marlowe, who is also a shoe maker and church warden, apologised for his son and assured us there will be no repeat of the fighting on our streets. "Kit's a little bit hotheaded," he said.

Again Christopher escaped without punishment – and again he didn't learn. His next big fight was going to be his last one.

In May 1593 he was in trouble. Deep trouble. Early that month posters had been pinned to a church gate in Broad Street, London. The poster told Londoners that they should throw the Dutch traders out of the country by force. It was telling people to riot and kill – and it was signed "Tamburlaine" – the name of the hero in Kit Marlowe's great play!

Kit Marlowe was not suspected of writing this poster but his friend, Thomas Kyd, was arrested and tortured. Thomas Kyd was also a playwright. When officers searched Kyd's room they found a letter that attacked the Christian Church. The torturers asked Kyd, "Whose is this?"

Kyd replied, "It's not mine! Don't blame me. It was left there by Kit Marlowe when we shared a room two years ago!"

Kit Marlowe was in trouble. He was arrested in Canterbury and brought back to London. The charges were serious. Marlowe could have been executed if he was found guilty.

The court decided to set Marlowe free until the date of his trial. But Marlowe never went to trial. His third knife-fight was his last...

THE
DEPTFORD DAILY NEWS

• 31 MAY 1593 •

"Kit" Career Cut Short

Yesterday the playwright Christopher "Kit" Marlowe died in a house on Deptford Strand in a horrific accident.

THE HOUSE OF HORROR

At 10:00 A.M. on Wednesday morning Marlowe (29) met three friends named Skeres, Frizer and Poley, at Mrs. Bull's house in Deptford Strand. It appears they spent the day walking in the garden and talking.

At 6:00 P.M. they entered the house and had supper. An hour later Mrs. Bull was called to the room where she saw the playwright lying on the floor, his head soaked in blood from a wound to the eye.

Frizer was bleeding from wounds to his head. He claimed that Marlowe had attacked him with a dagger and accidentally stabbed himself in the eye.

From previous page...

MR. SHAKESPEARE
"VERY UPSET"

William Danby, coroner to the royal household, will hold an inquest into this curious death.

Playwright William Shakespeare said today that he was very upset by the death of such a great writer. "It is sad to think of all the plays he'll never write," the Stratford writer said.

The inquest was held the next day, 1 June 1593. The report told the story of Frizer, Skeres and Poley. But the great story-teller, Marlowe, was not around to give his side of the "accident"

The report said the following. Can you see why it is a little suspicious? Can you see why some people have been saying ever since that the story of an accident was a lie? Read it and see what you think...

REPORT
into the Death
OF
Christopher
MARLOWE

IT happened that Christopher Marlowe met with a certain Ingram Frizer and Nicholas Skeres and Robert Poley, at a house in Deptford. They met at the tenth hour before noon, on the thirtieth day of May, in the thirty-fifth year of the reign of Queen Elizabeth in a room in the house of a certain Eleanor Bull, widow. They passed the time together there and dined. After dinner they walked together quietly in the garden belonging to the house. At the sixth hour after noon they returned from the garden to the room and ate supper together there.

After supper Ingram Frizer and Christopher Marlowe argued and exchanged angry words since they could not agree about the payment of the sum of pence - the reckoning.

Christopher Marlowe was lying on the bed in the room where they had supped. He moved

The Coroner's Office, Greenwich Palace, London

Mr. Marlowe

Mr Marlowe lying on bed

bed

Mr Frizer

Mr Skeres

Mr Skeres' dirty hair

they supped on good mutton chops and ale

Mrs Bull's cat

Mr Frizer's dagger

Dead mouse

crumbs

Mr Poley

This diagram drawn by Stephen Culpepper, Junior Clerk, Coroner's Office

angrily against Ingram Frizer as they exchanged these angry words. Ingram Frizer was sitting in the room with his back towards the bed where Christopher Marlowe was lying. He was sitting at a table with Nicholas Skeres and Robert Poley sitting on either side so that he could in no way escape.

Christopher Marlowe suddenly drew Ingram Frizer's dagger which was at his back and with the same dagger Christopher Marlowe gave Ingram Frizer two wounds on the head to the length of two inches and the depth of a quarter of an inch. Ingram Frizer, in fear of being slain and sitting between the other two in such a way that he could not escape, struggled with Christopher Marlowe in self-defence. He tried to get the dagger back from him and it so happened that, in the struggle, he gave Christopher Marlowe a wound over his right eye to the depth of two inches and a width of one inch. From this wound the said Christopher Marlowe then and there instantly died.

Spot anything odd? Here are some questions without answers:

Why didn't Marlowe attack with his own dagger? We know he always had one ready when he got into a fight. It would be difficult to get a dagger from the belt of a man sitting at a table.

? If Frizer was trapped at the table then Marlowe could have stabbed him through the back if he'd wanted to. Frizer escaped with two cuts. Why didn't Marlowe kill him?

? Why did Frizer have his back to Marlowe if they were supposed to be arguing? You don't usually argue with someone standing behind you.

? If Marlowe had the dagger gripped to stab someone then it's not easy to twist it so it is pointing at your own eye. Was Marlowe holding the dagger in such a way that he could beat Frizer over the head with the handle? That would make a stab in the eye easier.

? Was the argument over the bill really something to fight and die for? Or was there something else? What had the men been talking about for eight hours?

? Why was Frizer released from prison just four weeks after stabbing Marlowe? Did he have important friends who made sure he went free? What did he do for those friends? Kill Marlowe, perhaps? A queen's pardon dated 28 June said, "We are therefore moved by pity to pardon Ingram Frizer for the death of Christopher Marlowe."

Here are some answers. All are possible.

Three against one

We know that Marlowe, Frizer, Poley and Skeres were all working for Elizabeth's government as spies. The argument was not about who paid the bill. It was about their spying business. Marlowe argued with the other three but the reason he couldn't kill Frizer was that the other two ganged up on him. In the struggle Marlowe was killed by all three men. The government arranged for Frizer to go free. If they hadn't then Frizer might have given away some of his spy secrets.

Murder plot

There was no attack by Marlowe and no struggle. Marlowe had enemies in the spying business who wanted to see him dead. The enemies paid Skeres, Poley and Ingram to kill the playwright. After a big meal with lots of wine Kit Marlowe lay down on the

bed to rest. As soon as he closed his eyes Frizer crept over to him and slipped his dagger into Marlowe's eye. The other two agreed to say it was an accident.

Escape!

Kit Marlowe did not die. He was going to prison for a long time for his problems with the Kyd letter. His spy friends spent all day plotting some way to get him free and decided it would be best to fake Marlowe's death. Using fake stage blood they made it look like Marlowe had been stabbed in the eye. A friendly doctor agreed to say Marlowe was dead. The playwright hid for the rest of his life in Canterbury or in Europe. Some people even believe he went on writing plays but put another writer's name on them. The name he used was William Shakespeare!

Whichever one you believe about his death, there is one thing certain. Christopher 'Kit' Marlowe led a truly terribly dangerous life!

Quick Quill pens

There were no printing machines in Bede's day. By Marlowe's time there were books being printed but he would still have to use a pen made from a feather to write his scripts, just as Bede had nine hundred years before.

Bede wrote on the leather from a calf's belly. The monastery kept a large herd to keep the monks sup-

1. TAKE A SEAGULL'S FEATHER OR A GOOSE FEATHER.

this kind, fool!

2. WASH IT IN HOT WATER THEN DRY IT.

3. TRIM OFF THE FEATHERY PART WITH A SHARP KNIFE TO LEAVE ONLY THE CENTRAL SHAFT.

4. CUT THE END SQUARE. CUT AWAY THE BACK OF THE NIB THEN MAKE A SLIT HALF A CENTIMETRE UP THE SHAFT.

BE VERY CAREFUL NOT TO CUT YOURSELF!

5. DIP IT IN THE INK AND WRITE.

plied. Bede could scrape the ink off the leather if he made a mistake.

Kit Marlowe had paper but it was very expensive. He couldn't afford to make too many mistakes. Shakespeare made very few mistakes and wasted hardly any paper - we don't know how good Marlowe was with a pen.

But you can find out how good you would be! Make this quill pen. You may find Marlowe had more problems than just street fights – writing was a big problem!

Note: You can write on paper. Do NOT go out and kill a calf so you can use its belly-leather to write on!

Charles Dickens

1812 - 1870

THE VICTORIAN VICTIM

Christopher Marlowe lived in London when it was dangerous, dirty and unhealthy. Poor people lived in dark and narrow streets. If disease didn't kill them then the criminals might. Anyone who lived past 30 was old.

History teachers tell us that the 1666 Great Fire of London destroyed the ancient slums and a new, better city rose from the ashes. Marlowe's stinking city disappeared forever. Don't believe it!

The writer Charles Dickens lived there two hundred years after the Great Fire and there were still stinking streets that turned to liquid mud in the winter and houses where people slept forty to a room. There were still dreadful diseases, cruel crimes and the pitiful poor.

How do we know? Because Charles Dickens described it for us.

How did he know? Because he lived through it and saw the suffering for himself.

Of course Dickens was a story-teller. People read his books because they were entertaining, fascinating and gripping. But those readers were also made to "think" about the horrors of the cities. And the readers became angry and made the government change things. That is the power of a great writer. A great writer can change the world we live in.

DICKENS' LONDON

Charles Dickens never wrote his life story - though parts of David Copperfield are similar to his own early life. If he had told his story, it would have been as truly terrible as any of his books. This is what he might have written in his notebook on his twelfth birthday...

Happy birthday, Charles

7 February 1824
This morning I wake with a scream from some dreadful dream. My hair is sticking to my forehead with the sweat yet the room is cold as the graveyard clay. I've had these nightmares for years now, ever since Father hired a nurse called Mary Weller to look after me, my brothers and my sisters.

Somewhere outside the window this morning I hear the creaking of cartwheels and the sucking sound of horses' hooves in the mud of the street. I haven't a clock but I know people are stirring and it must be time to get up and walk the four miles to work.

In the room there are soft snores of two other boys. I don't want to light a candle and disturb them. Instead I pull off my night-shirt and fumble for the clothes that I've folded and placed on the chair by the bed. It takes me ten

minutes to dress and grope my way
across the room to the door. It won't
be light for an hour or so yet.

I stumble downstairs into the
kitchen, splash freezing water onto my
face from a jug by the sink and snatch
at a penny cottage loaf and a
pennyworth of milk for my breakfast.
I'm keeping another loaf and cheese on
a shelf in the cupboard for my supper. I
try to wash my hands but the grey

stains won't come out though I scrub them till they're sore.

It's barely light as I step out into the street where the morning air hits me in the face like the slap of a wet hand. The smell of the river stings my nostrils. As householders light their fires the chimneys start to smoke. In the heavy, misty air the soot falls like snow-flakes and fills my mouth with the taste of ashes. It grows lighter so I know the sun is up there somewhere. I keep my head down and begin the four mile walk to Warren's Blacking Factory in the twisted, tumbling, cobwebbed house by the river at Hungerford Stairs. My legs drag and I feel sure they are refusing to take me to the torturous work.

It might not be so bad if I was been born to it. But just a year ago my life was so different. In spite of Mary Weller's tales of terror we were a large and happy family. But last year we moved to London. My father lost his money and was locked away in a debtors' prison. I'd be there with him now if I hadn't been offered the job in Warren's Blacking Factory.

Six shillings a week, they pay me. Twelve pence for each day of drudgery. If they paid me a penny for every tear I shed then I'd be a rich man. I visit my father every Sunday in his prison and he weeps too when he sees me. He

The result is misery, Charles.

65

tells me about money. "Charles," he groans, "Oh, Charles. Always remember this lesson. If a man earns twenty pounds a year and spends nineteen pounds, nineteen shillings and sixpence then the result is happiness. But if he spends twenty pounds and sixpence – ah, then the result is misery!" And he looks towards the fireplace in the grim, grey cell. There is a brick at each side of the grate so the fire will not burn too much coal.

We don't even have sixpence now. I had been enjoying my education. But when Father went bankrupt we were forced to sell my books. They even sold my bed.

In the early morning light I can see figures scurrying across the muddy banks of the river. Someone has counted the sewers that run into the River Thames and they say there are 369. All that sewage, apart from the waste from the tar factories, the tanning factories and the slaughter houses on its banks. Yet the "mudlarks", children no older than me, are crawling like crabs at the sewer outlets looking for something useful washed down. Something they can sell.

And the pickpockets are already out on the street corners, watching me with their hooded eyes as I walk along the soot-stained, mud-slimed pavements. They live in gangs in the narrow tangle of terraces they call "rookeries". They never bother me for

they know I've nothing left for them to steal. The Bow Street runners catch them sometimes. And sometimes the gang leaders are caught and executed outside the prisons.

Just last week I was late for work because crowds blocked the streets and stopped me getting through. They'd gathered to watch the hanging of someone on a rough scaffold rigged outside the prison gate. I had to watch as the rope went round the villain's neck and the crowd fell silent as he said his farewell words. A hood was pulled over his head, the trapdoor dropped and the crowd cheered wildly.

I was late for work that morning. They say there was a crowd of 30,000 people there to watch the execution. They also say that more people died in the crowd than died on the scaffold. Cut-throat robbers roamed through the crowd and stole and killed and escaped in the confusion. When will they learn? When will they hang these

people quietly inside the prison walls? But this morning I'm not late for work. I'm on time. And Mr Warren himself is waiting at the door.

"Dickens," he says and looks down from under his tall top hat. "Dickens, your father is freed."

"From jail?" I ask.

"Where else?" he sneers. "It seems your family inherited some money. He's paid his debts and he's free."

I turn away from the factory workshop where I've spent endless hours putting labels on the blacking bottles. "Where are you going?" he asks sharply.

"Home to Camden Town. Home to see my father."

"You can't go home! You're paid to work here, boy!" he roars. "If you go off now then I'll see you do not get another farthing even though you're owed three days!"

"I don't care!" I cry and turn and run. It seems as if the sun has broken through the grimy clouds and is shining down just for me. I've never known such happiness in all my life.

I run all the way home and tear through the door where my brothers and sisters are scampering round excitedly. My father is sitting beside a flickering fire and drinking wine and eating biscuits. He looks up and he smiles, "Ah, Charles, my boy. You've come to welcome your old father home, have you?"

I don't believe I can see him clearly for all the tears that are flooding to my eyes. But I hear my mother clearly. I hear the door open. I heard the other children fall silent and I hear her say, "Charles? What are you doing here? You should be at work!"

I turn and look up at her frozen face as hard as Mary Weller's. "I thought — I thought that — now that father's free —"

"Get back to work. We can't afford to have too many idle children hanging round this house. Get back to work. You're eleven years old and that's quite old enough to earn yourself a wage."

I stumble to my feet and look up at her loveless face. "No, mother," I say softly. "I'm twelve years old. Today's my birthday. Perhaps you have forgotten."

I walk out of the room and back onto the bustling streets. Tonight I'll go back home. I know just two things. I will never

go back to that Blacking factory — and I will never forgive my mother.

I remember the horror of Mary Weller. She had a red face and yellow eyes glinted in the candle-light as she told her bedtime tales. Tales of terror meant to send us to sleep. She told us stories about Captain Murderer. "Oh how he loved his wives!" she crowed. "He loved them baked and toasted, boiled or stewed but he loved them most of all in pies!" Then she cackled and tucked us into our bed. Worst of all were the nights when she told us how Captain Murderer met his end, tortured to death by rats.

She would blow out the candle and leave me lying in the dark. Every creak in the old house was a rat coming to chew on my cheeks. Six years later I am still having the dream and still waking up with cold sweat sticking my night-shirt to my back.

But even Mary Weller is nothing compared to a loveless mother.

Happy birthday, Charles.

Charles Dickens never did go back to the Blacking Factory – and he never did forgive his mother for trying to send him back.

He never forgot those bleak days either. He created some wonderful characters in his books, but his greatest character is the city of London itself.

Charles Dickens wanted to change the cruelty and the misery of life for many British people – after all, he had suffered it himself. Do you know how bad life in the Victorian world was?

Try this test.

Hard times

1   In 1837 Charles Dickens heard reports of cruelty in Bowes Academy, a Yorkshire school for unwanted boys. It was run by William Shaw. Dickens visited the school and watched Shaw at work. He then created the villainous headmaster Wackford Squeers in his book Nicholas Nickleby. Everybody knew that Wackford Squeers was really William Shaw. The publication of the book ruined Shaw's business. He died in 1850. What was the worst that Shaw's boys suffered?

A They were given detention for an hour for talking in class	◯
B They were shouted at till they cried	◯
C They were starved and beaten so badly that they went blind	◯

2   Charles Dickens hated the Workhouse system. Very poor people were not given money to help them live; instead they were forced to go to the local workhouse which was little better than a prison. There they would work endlessly and live in terrible conditions. Dickens described the horrors of the workhouse in his Oliver Twist. Workhouses were slowly improved after the book was published and after a famous riot in a workhouse at Andover. What started it?

A   Someone found a scrap of meat on a bone and the workers fought for it   ◯

B   The workhouse was too comfortable and poor people fought to get into it   ◯

C   The beds were too hard and the workers wanted softer straw   ◯

3   In Oliver Twist the writer also looked at the criminal "underworld" of London. Oliver Twist was a child when he was taken in by Fagin's criminal gang. This was a dangerous life for a child. In 1833 a nine year-old boy pushed a stick through the cracked window of a shop and stole two

pence worth of printers' ink. He was caught and taken before a judge. What did the judge sentence him to?

A To 3 years in prison

B To be executed by hanging

C To be transported to Australia for 10 years

4   Charles Dickens was a believer in justice. In 1868 two street thieves tried to rob him. He chased them through the streets, captured them and made sure they went to prison. This was a reckless thing to do because thieves often had a lot of sympathy from the poor people of London. When the London Police Force started work in 1829 you'd expect the public to have been a bit more helpful. What did children do when they saw a policeman in the street?

A Run out and offer to clean their boots for a penny	○
B Run and hide because they were afraid	○
C Sing a song to warn any local criminals that the police were around	○

5   As Dickens grew more famous he began to travel around reading chapters from his books and acting out some of the popular characters - he loved to act the villains. He went to America, a country he liked. But there were some things about America he hated and wrote about. He hated the way the Americans kept slaves. He also hated their habit of...

A Drinking coffee	○
B Spitting	○
C Carrying guns	○

Answers

1 – C. Two boys went blind after years of Shaw's treatment. Yet some of the local people of Bowes thought that Dickens had been unfair to Shaw. They dedicated a window to him in the local church after his death.

It wasn't only teachers who were harsh. Priests often helped in running schools that were attached to their church. One girl told this truly terrible tale –

"Every Monday morning the priest came to each class and asked us who had missed church the day before. I always had to miss Sunday because Sunday was washing day and we only had one lot of clothes. So, week by week we admitted our absence and were given the strap for it. We should have been able to explain but we were ashamed to give the real reason. Once, just once, I answered back.

"Don't you know," the priest said, "that God loves you and wants to see you in His house on Sundays?"

"But if he loves us, why does he want us to get the strap on Monday?" I asked.

I don't remember what the priest said, but I do know I got a double load of stripes when he'd gone"

2 – A. The workers had the job of grinding old bones up. One batch of bones arrived with a little meat still clinging to them and the starving workers fought to get their hands on these scraps. A report of the 1850s said:

"The bone pickers are the dirtiest of all the inmates of our workhouse; I have seen them take a bone from the dung heap and gnaw it while reeking hot with the process of decay. Bones from which the meat has been cut raw, and which still had thin strips of flesh sticking to them, they scraped carefully with their knives and put the bits, no matter how befouled with dirt, into a wallet or pocket. They have told me that, whether in broth or grilled, they were the most savoury dish that could be imagined. These creatures are often hardly human in appearance, they have no

Look! Dinner!

human tastes or understanding, nor even human feelings, for they revelled in the filth which we expect to see in dogs and other lower animals but which to us is sickening to us."

Charles Dickens' most famous scene is of Oliver Twist in the workhouse and begging for more food.

| 3 – B. | The boy was sentenced to death, though the sentence was later reduced to imprisonment. The same thing happened to a 13 year-old boy who stole a spoon in 1801, an eight year old girl for a small theft in 1808 and a nine year-old boy who started a fire in 1831. Dickens was actually in favour of these harsh punishments and the hangings. But he did think hangings should take place behind the prison walls, and not in public. In 1856 the law was changed and hangings outside the prison walls stopped. In 1846 he wrote to The Daily News newspaper ...

"I was present myself at the execution of Courvoisier. I was purposely on the spot from midnight of the night before, and was near witness to the whole process of the building of the scaffold, the gathering of the crowd, the gradual swelling of numbers with the coming of the day, the hanging of the man, the cutting of the body down and the removal of it to prison. From the moment of my arrival I did not see any suitable emotion in any of the immense crowd. No sorrow, no terror, no dislike, no seriousness – nothing but indecency, frivolity, drunkenness and vice in fifty other shapes. I thought it was impossible that I could feel so disgusted by my fellow-creatures."

It wasn't the hangings he minded – it was the behaviour of the spectators.

4 – C. The new police force was the idea of the government minister Sir Robert Peel, so the police were known as "Peelers" at first. The children would sing:

> *I spy blue, I spy black*
> *I spy a peeler in a shiny hat!*

The hats were tall top hats to protect the policeman from being beaten over the head. They also wore high, stiff collars to stop someone creeping up behind them, throwing a rope around their throat and strangling them. But still they weren't safe.

The police had only been working in London for a year when PC Grantham was stabbed to death while he was trying to break up a fight.

Even the upper classes hated the police. Earl Waldegrave once joined a friend to hold a policeman on the ground while his coach ran over him. The policeman survived but was too badly injured to ever work again.

5 – B. Dickens was shocked when he met the US President and noticed a large container for men to spit into - a spittoon. He also noticed that a lot of men missed the spittoon! He hated walking down a town street and dodging the spit as men spat out of open windows. His wife spent a night on a

stage coach journey suffering a man spattering her. He wrote:

"On a train journey I looked out of the window. The flashes of saliva flew so often that it looked as if they were ripping open feather beds. In the courts of law the judge has his spittoon on the bench, the lawyers have their, the witness has his, the prisoner his and the usher his. The jury are three men to a spittoon (or spit-box as they are called here) and the spectators in the gallery have theirs. There are spitboxes in every steamboat, bar-room, public dining room, house, office and public place no matter what it may be. In hospitals students are asked to use the spit-boxes and not spit on the stairs. I have twice seen gentlemen at evening parties in New York, turn aside when they were not talking and spit upon the carpet."

The death of Dickens

Charles Dickens lived a lonely, pitiful life when his father went to prison. He was quite sure he never wanted to suffer like that when he grew older.

He worked hard to be a success. He taught himself shorthand so he could become a newspaper reporter. When he wasn't doing newspaper work he was writing stories and had his first one published when he was 21.

He became very popular and earned a lot of money but he couldn't stop working. He travelled around giving talks and kept going even though he was ill and they exhausted him.

By 1870 he was 58 years old and worn out. He had written fourteen novels as well as a huge number of stories and articles. He could afford to retire but he drove himself on and on. On 9 June that year he died.

Charles Dickens is as famous as any writer of the English language - and so are his curious characters. But, in the end, it was fame that killed him – fame – and the fear of going back to those dark days of life in Warren's Blacking warehouse.

Sometimes writers can suffer truly terrible lives of their own.

TRULY TERRIBLE TALES

INVENTORS

People invent things for all kinds of reasons: to save lives, kill their enemies – or get themselves out of trouble! This book tells the remarkable stories of real-life inventors with ideas of their own:

Ancient Greek Archimedes, creator of the deadly ship-smasher...

Leonardo da Vinci, Renaissance genius – so brilliant, it's scary...

Tudor inventor Sir John Harington, who flushes away a royal stink...

and Joseph Lister, who sticks a knife into Queen Victoria!

85

TRULY TERRIBLE TALES

SCIENTISTS

If you think today's scientists are eccentric, wait till you find out about the dotty and dangerous ideas of four boffins from the past!

Aristotle, the Ancient Greek who thinks that maggots grow out of rotting flesh...

Mad medieval monk **Roger Bacon,** who discovers gunpowder by accident. Ooops!

Creepy **John Dee,** Tudor scientist – or wicked magician?

Francis Galton, Victorian thinker whose ideas led to death and suffering for millions.

TRULY TERRIBLE TALES

EXPLORERS

What makes someone risk everything to sail off into the unknown? In this book, you can read the amazing stories of four real-life adventurers:

Brave **Pytheas**, the Ancient Greek. Can he sail to the end of the world without falling off?

Marco Polo, medieval sailor. He says he's been to China _ but is he lying?

Tudor toff, **Sir Walter Raleigh**, who discovers the potato, then loses his head...

and fearless **Florence Baker**, Victorian explorer, who sees her own grave being dug!

ORDER FORM

0 340 66724 9 Truly Terrible Tales: Writers   £3.99 ☐

0 340 66722 2 Truly Terrible Tales: Inventors   £3.99 ☐

0 340 66723 0 Truly Terrible Tales: Scientists   £3.99 ☐

0 340 66721 4 Truly Terrible Tales: Explorers   £3.99 ☐

All Hodder Children's Books are available at your local bookshop or newsagent, or can be ordered direct from the publisher. Just tick the titles you want and fill in the form below. Prices and availability are subject to change without notice.

Hodder Children's Books Cash Sales Dept
Bookpoint, 39 Milton Park, Abingdon, Oxon OX14 4TD, UK

If you have a credit card, you may order by telephone on (01235) 831700

Please enclose a cheque or postal order made payable to Bookpoint Ltd to the value of the cover price, plus the following for postage and packing:

UK and BFPO: £1.00 for the first book, 50p for the second book, and 30p for each additional book ordered up to a maximum charge of £3.00. Overseas and Eire: £2.00 for the first book, £1.00 for the second book, and 50p for each additional book.

Name ....

Address ....

....

If you would prefer to pay by credit card, please complete:

Please debit my Visa / Access / Diner's Card / American Express (delete as applicable) card number:

Signature ....

Expiry date ....